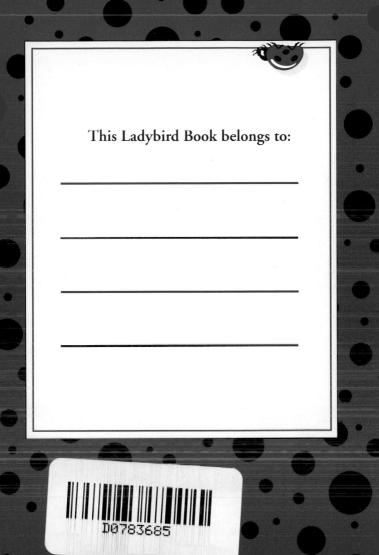

This Ladybird Book belongs to:

_____

_____

_____

_____

D0783685

Retold by Audrey Daly
Illustrated by Peter Stevenson

Cover illustration by Thea Kliros

Copyright © Ladybird Books USA 1996

All rights reserved. No part of this publication may be reproduced or transmitted in
any form or by any means, electronic or mechanical, including photocopy,
recording, or any information storage and retrieval system now known or to be
invented, without permission in writing from publisher, except by a reviewer who
wishes to quote brief passages in connection with a review written for inclusion in a
magazine, newspaper, or broadcast.

Originally published in the United Kingdom by Ladybird Books Ltd © 1993

First American edition by Ladybird Books USA
An Imprint of Penguin USA Inc.
375 Hudson Street, New York, New York 10014

Printed in Great Britain
10 9 8 7 6 5 4 3 2 1

ISBN 0–7214–5622–7

FAVORITE TALES

Hansel
and
Gretel

nce upon a time, a boy named Hansel and his sister Gretel lived with their father and stepmother in a cottage near a forest.

They were so poor that sometimes they did not have enough to eat.

One day the children heard their stepmother say to their father, "Tomorrow we must take the children deep into the forest and leave them there. Otherwise, we shall starve."

Gretel was frightened, but Hansel had a plan. That night, when everyone was asleep, he crept outside and filled his pockets with shiny white pebbles.

The next morning, when the family went into the forest, Hansel walked more slowly than the others. When no one was looking, he dropped his pebbles along the path.

Deep in the forest, their stepmother left the children by themselves. She told them to wait until someone came to fetch them. They waited until it grew dark, but no one came.

At last the moon rose. Hansel showed Gretel the pebbles he had dropped. They shined white in the moonlight and showed the children the way home.

When the tired, hungry children arrived back at the cottage, their father was very glad to see them.

But their stepmother was angry. The next day she told their father that they would have to take the children into the forest again.

"This time we must see that they cannot find their way home!" she said.

That night, while everyone slept, Hansel got up to collect more pebbles. He tried to open the door, but his stepmother had locked it and hidden the key.

In the morning, before they all set off, their stepmother gave the two children a small piece of bread for their lunch.

They had not gone very far before Hansel again began walking more slowly than the others.

"Hansel! Why are you so slow?" his stepmother shouted. "Hurry up!"

"I am only saying goodbye to my friends the birds," said Hansel. But he was really stopping to drop bread crumbs along the path.

When the family had gone deep into the forest, the father lit a small fire for his children. He told them to wait beside it until someone came to fetch them.

The children waited until it grew dark, but no one came.

In the moonlight, Hansel and Gretel looked for the trail of bread crumbs to lead them home.

But there was not a single crumb on the path. The birds had eaten them all!

The children tried to find their way out of the forest, but they did not know which path to take. They were lost.

Hansel and Gretel were tired and frightened and very, very hungry. They did not know where to go or what to do next.

Suddenly, Gretel cried, "Hansel,
look!" Just ahead of them was a
strange little house made of cakes
and gingerbread, with a roof of
sugary icing.

Laughing with pleasure, the children
broke off bits of the house and began
to eat.

Slowly, the door of the little
house opened and an old woman
stepped out.

"Hello, children," she said, smiling. "Come inside and I will give you food and a warm place to sleep."

The children went into the house. The old woman gave them some delicious cookies and milk. She even had two little beds for them to sleep in.

Hansel and Gretel were happy to have met such a kind woman. They did not know that she was really a wicked witch who liked to eat little children!

The next day the Witch put Gretel to
work scrubbing the floors. Then she
took poor Hansel and locked him in
a cage.

Every morning the Witch, who had
very poor eyesight, told Hansel to
hold out his finger so that she could
feel how fat he had grown.

And each day clever Hansel held out
a skinny chicken bone instead.

"Not nearly fat enough yet," the
Witch would mutter.

Day after day, Hansel kept holding out the skinny chicken bone instead of his finger.

Finally, the Witch grew impatient. "I will wait no longer! He *must* be fat enough by now," she said one morning. "Today I will cook Hansel and eat him. Gretel, light the oven!"

With tears in her eyes, Gretel did as she was told.

"Gretel, climb in and see if the oven is hot," the Witch ordered.

But Gretel was sure that the Witch was trying to trick her. "I can't climb into the oven," she said. "I'm much too big."

"Of course you can," said the Witch angrily. "Look, I will show you." And she bent down and stuck her head into the oven.

Gretel did not waste a second. She gave the witch a push and slammed the oven door. The Witch screamed with rage, but she could not get out.

When Gretel was sure the Witch was
dead, she unlocked Hansel's cage
and let her brother out.

"We're free!" she cried. "Let's
go home!"

Before they left, Hansel and Gretel
searched the Witch's house. In the
attic, they found chests full of pearls
and rubies and diamonds.

"We must take these home to
Father," said Hansel.

As the children set off, Hansel
saw a white dove flying high
above. "One of my friends is
showing us the way!" he cried.

Soon the children saw their own cottage through the trees. Their father was overjoyed to see them.

"Your stepmother has gone, and she is never coming back," he said, hugging his children.

When their father saw the jewels, he could not believe his eyes. "We're rich!" he cried. "And we shall never be parted again."

And they never were.

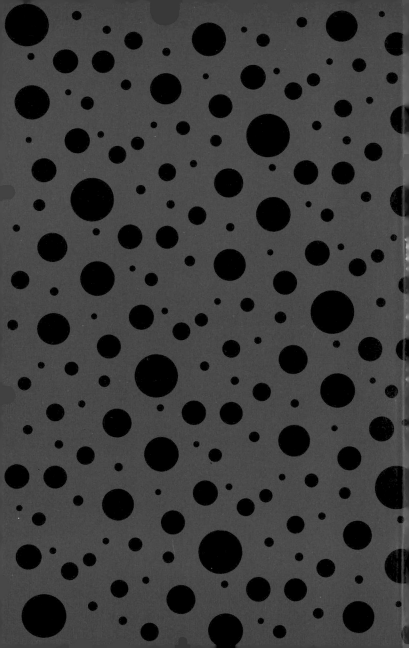